The Life and Exploits of Three-Finger'd Jack

The Life and Exploits of Three-Finger'd Jack

The Terror of Jamaica

William Burdett

MINT EDITIONS

The Life and Exploits of Three-Finger'd Jack: The Terror of Jamaica was first published in 1801.

This edition published by Mint Editions 2021.

ISBN 9781513211954 | E-ISBN 9781513210759

Published by Mint Editions®

 MINT
EDITIONS

minteditionbooks.com

Publishing Director: Jennifer Newens
Design & Production: Rachel Lopez Metzger
Project Manager: Micaela Clark
Typesetting: Westchester Publishing Services

This daring marauder, whose real name was MANSONG, and who, for a considerable time, kept all *Jamaica* in awe, was of a bold and martial appearance; he was above the common stature, and his limbs well shapen and athletic; his face was rather long; his eyes keen and penetrating; his nose was not like the generality of blacks, squat and flat, but rather aqueline; and his skin remarkably clear. His countenance was very expressive; and even a look of reproach from him would frequently make the overseers of the plantation tremble, as they smote him for neglect of duty; while the steadiness of his manners, and firm intrepidity of his mind, commanded the reverence of those who, like him, wielded the servile spade.

Onowauhee, the father of our hero, dwelt at *Simbing*, in the interior of *Africa*, adjoining the country of the *Moors. Simbing* is scarcely a day's journey from *Jarra*, a large Moorish town, situated at the bottom of some rocky hills. He was in the decline of years; and his cattle were frequently stolen by the Moorish robbers, who came in large parties, and plundered the peaceful inhabitants.

Mansong was now grown to manhood, and took upon himself the protection of his father's property. One day, a large party of the *Moors* came down, and drove before them the finest from amongst the herds. The people stood affrighted at the doors of their huts; but *Mansong* lifted high his javelin, and struck to the heart the leader of the robbers, who fell dead upon the plain. The Moors were determined to resent this outrage, as they termed it, and sent back the javelin; the aim was good; and *Mansong* fell to the ground, bathed in his blood. The inhabitants set up a loud scream, and the Moors drove off with their booty. *Mansong* was borne to his father's hut upon the shoulders of his countrymen. When they had laid him upon a mat, all the spectators joined in lamenting his fate, by screaming and howling in the most piteous manner. *Onowauhee* tore his hair, in the bitterness of grief; and casting himself on the body of his son, he expired in sight of the bewildered spectators!

Mansong was not, however, deprived of life.—The javelin had pierced his breast, and a great effusion of blood succeeded. This occasioned a fainting-fit, from which he shortly recovered. The astonished people made frantic gestures, in token of their joy; and being of the Mahometan persuasion, exclaimed, *"La illah el ellah Mahamet rasowl allahi."*—"There is but one God, and Mahomet is his prophet."

They administered some refreshment to *Mansong*, carefully concealing from him the death of his father; he soon fell into a refreshing sleep, and they withdrew. The body of *Onowauhee* was now borne away, and deposited in a place of worship, dedicated to Mahomet, where it was watched for three days by those unenlightened people, thinking their good prophet would restore him to life again; but in this they were disappointed; and on the fourth day he was buried.

Mansong was now perfectly recovered, and determined to revenge the death of his father, whom he for a long time bewailed in the bitterness of filial grief. He collected his countrymen, and exhorted them to rush upon the *Moors,* and repair the losses they daily sustained; but the people of *Simbing* loved peace, and could not then be prevailed upon.

The fiery soul of *Mansong* was not defeated by a cool refusal. Another opportunity soon presented itself; he again pictured to them the horrors and calamities they were daily exposed to, and again exhorted them to revenge. The youths now complied; and *Mansong* led them to join the King of *Kaarta,* who was just then waging war with the perfidious King of *Bambarra.* This King beheld with a jealous eye the growing prosperity of the King of *Kaarta,* and availed himself of the following trifling opportunity to declare hostilities against that country.

The Moorish robbers, who as frequently made incursions into *Bambarra* as *Kaarta,* had stolen from the former an immense drove of their finest cattle, which they fold to a Dooty, or chief man of a town, in *Kaarta.* The people of *Bambarra* gaining a knowledge of their cattle, claimed them of the Dooty, who refused to restore them; upon which, they complained to their King. Glad of the opportunity, he sent a messenger, escorted by a party of horsemen, to *Daisy,* King of *Kaarta,* to inform him that the King of *Bambarra,* with nine thousand men, would visit *Kemmoo,* the chief town, in the dry season; and to desire that *Daisy* would direct his slaves to sweep the houses, and have everything ready for their accommodation. The messenger concluded this insulting notification, by presenting the King with a pair of iron sandals, at the same time adding, that "until such time as *Daisy* had worn out those sandals in his flight, he should never be secure from the arrows of *Bambarra.*"

Daisy, after having consulted with his chief men about the best means of repelling so formidable an enemy, returned an answer of defiance; and caused to be written, in Arabic, upon a piece of thin board, a proclamation, which was suspended to a tree in the public square; and a number of aged men were sent to different places to explain it to the common people. It called upon all the friends of *Daisy* to join him immediately; but to such as had no arms, or were afraid to enter into the war, permission was given to retire into any of the neighbouring kingdoms; and it was added, that provided they observed a strict neutrality, they should always be welcome to return to their former habitations; if, however, they took any active part against *Kaarta,* they had then "broken the key of their hut, and could never again enter the door." Such was the expression. This proclamation was generally applauded; but many of the *Kaartans,* and, amongst others, the powerful tribes of *Joover* and *Kakaro,* availing themselves of the indulgent clause, retired from *Daisy's* dominions, and took refuge in *Ludamar* and *Rasson.*

By means of these desertions, *Daisy's* army was not so numerous as might have been expected; and when encamped at *Kemmoo,* the whole number of effective men did not exceed four thousand; but they were men of spirit and enterprize, and could be depended on.

Mansong, with his small troop from *Simbing,* had joined them; and their appearance was joyful to the heart of *Daisey. Mansong* had tutored his adventurous heroes in the art of war; had taught them evolutions which the King of *Kaarta* was unacquainted with; and he embraced, with all the fervor of his heart, so powerful an ally. He also undertook to discipline the men of *Kaarta,* and was unanimously chosen commander in chief.

Daisy now defied the malice of the powerful King of *Bambarra,* placing confidence in the valour of those few troops that were scarcely one-fourth the number of his foes, who now appeared before the town of *Kemmoo. Mansong* led his men to the field. The *Kaartans* became faint at heart when they beheld the numbers that were opposed to them; but their leader encouraged them by example; and the slaughter commenced!—The *Bambarrans* were mown down like blades of grass: but their numbers were great; and as often as a chasm was effected, it was filled by fresh troops. They visibly gained ground; and at length the men of *Kaarta* fled, with great slaughter.

Mansong now, with a corps of reserve, rushed upon the foe, and bore down all before his conquering arm. This encouraged the troops of *Kaarta,* who again appeared in the field, aiding those of *Simbing,* headed by the victorious *Mansong,* who fought like a tyger. His valour inspired his own men with courage; struck terror to the hearts of his foe; and he came off victorious!

When he returned from the fight, *Daisy,* with tears of gratitude, embraced him, and hailed him as a son. The *Bambarrans* retreated from *Kemmoo,* but in three days again appeared before the walls with redoubled force. *Mansong* knew it would be madness to resist them now, and therefore retreated to *Joko,* a town to the north-west of *Kemmoo,* whither he was followed by the King of *Bambarra*; he then, with his small troop, took refuge in a strong town called *Gedingooma,* situated in a hilly country, and surrounded with high stone-walls.

When *Daisy,* by command of *Mansong,* departed from *Joko,* his sons refused to accompany him; alledging, that "the singing-men would publish their disgrace, as soon as it should be known that he and his family had fled from *Joko* without firing a gun." They were therefore left behind, with a number of horsemen, to defend *Joko*; but, after many skirmishes, they were totally defeated, and one of *Daisy's* sons taken prisoner. The remainder fled to *Gedingooma,* which *Mansong* had fortified and stored with provisions, and where he determined to make his final stand.—The King of *Bambarra* finding that *Daisy* wished to avoid a pitched battle, placed a strong force at *Joko,* to watch his motions; and separating the remainder of his army into small detachments, ordered them to over-run the country, and seize the inhabitants before they had time to escape. These orders were executed with such promptitude, that in a few days they were scattered over the whole kingdom of *Kaarta.*

These proceedings were according to the wish of *Mansong,* who had prepared troops in private for their reception, and sent others to the kingdom of *Bambaara,* which, in a short time, became a scene of desolation; for the King having left it in an unguarded state, and dispersed his troops in small detachments to harrass the *Kaartans,* they were almost all cut off; while in *Bambarra* most of the poor inhabitants of the different towns and villages being surprised in the night, became an easy prey, and their corn and everything else which could be of use to the King, was burnt and destroyed.

During these transactions, the politic *Mansong* was employed in fortifying *Gedingooma.* This town is built in a narrow pass between two high mountains, having two gates, one towards *Kaarta* and the other towards *Jaffnoo.* The gate towards *Kaarta* was defended by *Mansong* in person, and that towards *Jaffnoo* was committed to the charge of *Daisy* and his sons. When the army of *Bambarra* approached the town, they made some attempts to storm it, but were always driven back with great loss; and finding *Mansong* more formidable than they expected, they resolved to cut off his supplies, and starve him into submission. For this purpose, therefore, their King, having sent a large party to *Bambarra* with the prisoners they had taken, and to assist his country, which was falling a sacrifice to his enemy, and having collected a considerable quantity of provisions, remained with his army two months in the vicinity of *Gedingooma,* without doing anything decisive. During this time, he was much harrassed by sallies from the besieged; and his stock of provisions, being nearly exhausted, he sent to *Ali,* the *Moorish* King of *Ludamar,* for two hundred horsemen, to enable him to make an attack upon the north-gate of the city, and afford him an opportunity of storming the place; but *Ali,* though he had made an agreement, at the commencement of the war, to afford him assistance, now refused to fulfil his engagement.

Mansong, at length, tired of this shilli-shalli fighting, issued with his men from the town, and gave battle to the *Bambarrans,* who were defeated with great loss. The King now sent to *Daisy* to treat for peace; and this worthy man, who loved the welfare of his people, immediately sent *Mansong,* accompanied by a small detachment of officers, to adjust the preliminaries. The *Bambarrans,* who were as eager as the *Kaartans* to have peace restored, loudly huzza'd as *Mansong* and his small troop entered *Sigo,* the town where the King waited to receive them. *Lubeg* (the King of *Bambarra*) saw with a joyful eye the leader of the *Kaartans* before him; and instantly devised a hellish scheme to ruin his foe, and terminate the glory of the great and warlike Mansong.

Peace being now agreed upon, joyful festivity reigned throughout *Bambarra,* and the ambassadors were requested to stay three days at *Sigo. Mansong,* although he wished to convey the news so eagerly sought for by his royal master, readily acquiesced; and *Lubeg* furnished them for three days with sumptuous entertainment. On the evening of the last, they were all invited to the palace, and the liquors of *Bambarra* were placed on the board; but *Mansong* requested permission to depart for *Kaarta. Lubeg* endeavoured to dissuade him from his purpose; and finding all intreaty vain, he gave the signal, and a large armed party rushed in.—"We are betrayed!" exclaimed *Mansong,* drawing his sword. The *Kaartans* fought most furiously; but overpowered by numbers, they were obliged to submit to their perfidious foes. *Mansong,* with gleaming fabre, like a tyger in the toils, darted on the foremost, and cleft him to the ground. The weapons of his adversaries clashed over his head; but he heeded not death, and struggled hard to break the chains that encircled him. He still fought, and his blood streamed around; till at length quite exhausted, he fell, covered with wounds; and four of his adversaries lay dead beside him. The others bound up his wounds, and, with the rest of his party, sent him to the caravan of a Slatee, or Slave-merchant.

Four hundred slaves were offered by *Daisy* for their release, but the offer was rejected; and, on the banks of the *Gambia*, they were fold to an *English* Captain, and brought to *Jamaica.*

(We have been thus particular in detailing the affairs of *Africa*, to shew in what estimation our hero was held in his native country, and that he had been inured to war.)

On the arrival of *Mansong* and his fellow-slaves in *Jamaica*, they were disposed of according to lot*. He was branded on the breast, and smiled upon the red-hot iron as it feared him; but he had vowed revenge, and called upon the God of his country to witness his vows of vengeance, on the European race. He had repeatedly received the lash of his employers on his bare shoulders; and as the blood trickled down his back, so did he resolve that for every drop, a white man's blood should sprinkle the plain.

Eighteen long tedious months had now elapsed since he was dragged from his native country—eighteen long months had heard his groans—and JACK (for so was he named after his arrival in *Jamaica*, and by which we shall in future call him) devised how to lash his persecutors with a rod of iron.

Amalkir, an Obeah practitioner, dwelt in a loathsome cave, far removed from the enquiring eye of the suspicious whites, in the *blue Mountains*; he was old and shrivelled; a disorder had contracted all his nerves, and he could scarcely crawl.—His cave was the dwelling-place or refuge of robbers; he encouraged them in their depradations, and gave them OBI, that they might fearless rush where danger stood. This obi was supposed to make them invulnerable to the attacks of the white men, and they placed implicit belief in its virtues.

---

* It fell to the lot of poor MANSONG to be disposed of to a Mr. K. of Port Royal, on whose plantation the slaves were treated with more severity than any other in the island.—The Editor of this History having some business to transact with the head Overseer of Mr. K.'s plantation, happened to call on him at the moment when Mansong was receiving a dozen lashes with a cart-whip, for staying FIVE MINUTES at dinner after the bell had called the slaves to work!—Those sanguinary punishments may, perhaps, in a great degree, account for his becoming a Zanga to his persecutors.

WILLIAM BURDETT

Before we proceed farther with the history of our hero, we shall present our readers with an authentic account of this practice, so prevalent in the British West Indies, and its fatal effects, corroborated by the authorities of Mr. *Bryan Edwards,* author of the *History of the West Indies,* Doctor *Moseley,* &c. &c.

The term *Obeah, Obiah,* or *Obia,* (for it is variously written) we conceive to be the adjective, and *Obe,* or *Obi,* the noun substantive; and that by the terms Obeah-men or women, are meant those who practise Obi. From the learned Mr. *Bryant's* commentary upon the word *Oph,* in his *Mythology,* Vol. I we obtain a very probable etymology of the term:—"A serpent, in the *Egyptian* language, was called *Ob,* or *Aub, Obion* is still the Egyptian name for a serpent. The woman at *Endor* is called *Oub,* or *Ob,* translated *Pythonissa;* and *Oubaois* was the name of the basilisk, or royal serpent; an emblem of the fun, and an ancient oracular Deity of *Africa.*"

This derivation, which applies to one particular sect, the remnant, probably, of a very celebrated religious order in remote ages, is now become in *Jamaica* the general term to denote those *Africans* who, in that island, practise witchcraft or sorcery; comprehending also the class of what are called *Mysal* men, or those who, by means of a narcotic potion, made with the juice of an herb, (said to be the branched calalue, or species of solanum) which occasions a trance, or profound sleep, of a certain duration, endeavour to convince the deluded spectators of their power to re-animate dead bodies.

As far as we are able to decide, from our own experience and information, while we lived on the island, and from the current testimony of all the negroes we have ever conversed with on the subject, the professors of Obi are, and always were, natives of *Africa,* and none other; and they have brought the science with them from thence to *Jamaica;* where it is so universally practised, that there are few of the large estates, possessing native *Africans,* which have not one or more of them. Those whose hoary heads, and a somewhat peculiarly harsh and forbidding aspect, together with some skill in plants of the medicinal and poisonous species, have qualified them for impositions on the weak and credulous, usually attract the greatest devotion and confidence. The negroes in general, whether Africans or Creoles, revere, consult, and fear them. To these oracles they resort, with the most implicit faith, upon all occasions, whether for the cure of disorders, the obtaining revenge for injuries or insults, the conciliating of favour, the discovery and punishment of the thief or adulterer, or the prediction of future events.

The trade which those impostors carry on is extremely lucrative; they manufacture and sell their Obies, adapted to different cases and at different prices; a veil of mystery is studiously thrown over their incantations, to which the midnight hours are allotted; and every precaution is taken to conceal them from the knowledge of the whites. The deluded negroes become the willing accomplices in this concealment; and the stoutest among them tremble at the very fight of the ragged bundle, the bottle, or the egg shells, which are stuck in the thatch or hung over the door of a hut, or upon the branch of a plaintain-tree, to deter marauders. In cases of poison, the natural effects of it are, by the ignorant negroes, ascribed entirely to the potent workings of Obi. The wiser negroes hesitate to reveal their suspicions, from a dread of incurring the terrible vengeance which is fulminated by the Obeah men against anyone who should betray them; it is, therefore, very difficult for the white proprietor to distinguish the obeah professor from any other negro on his plantations and so infatuated are the blacks in general, that but few instances occur of their having assumed courage enough to impeach those miscreants.

With minds so firmly prepossessed, they no sooner find Obi set for them near the door of their hut, or in the path leading to it, than they give themselves up for lost! When a negro is robbed of a hog or a fowl, he applies directly to an Obeah man or woman; it is then made known among his fellow blacks that obi is set for the thief; and as soon as the latter hears the dreadful news, his terrified imagination begins to work: no resource is left but in the superior skill of some more eminent Obeah man in the neighbourhood, who may counteract the magical operations of the other; but if no one can be found of higher rank and ability, or if, after gaining such an ally, he should still fancy himself affected, he presently falls into a decline, under the incessant horror of impending calamities. The slightest painful sensation in the head, the bowels, or any other part, or any casual hurt, confirms his apprehensions, and he believes himself the devoted victim of an invisible and irresistible agency. Sleep, appetite, and chearfulness forsake him; his strength decays; his disturbed imagination is continually haunted; his features wear the settled gloom of despondency; dirt, or any other unwholesome substance, becomes his only food; he contracts a morbid habit of body, and gradually sinks into the grave!

WILLIAM BURDETT

A negro, when taken ill, enquires of the Obeah man the cause of his sickness; whether it will prove mortal or not, and within what time he shall die or recover? The Oracle generally ascribes the distemper to the malice of some particular person, whom he names, and advises to set Obi for that person; but if no hopes are given of recovery, despair immediately takes place, which no medicine can remove, and death is the certain consequence!—Those anomalous symptoms which originate from causes deeply rooted in the mind, such as the terrors of Obi, or from poisons whose operations are flow and intricate, will baffle the most skilful physician.

Considering the multitude of occasions which provoke the negroes to exercise the power of Obi against each other, and the astonishing influence of this superstition upon their minds, we cannot but attribute a very considerable portion of the annual mortality among the negroes of Jamaica to this fascinating mischief.

The Obi is usually composed of a farrago of materials, (most of which are enumerated in the *Jamaica* Law, passed in 1760) viz. Grave-dirt, hair, teeth of sharks, alligators, and other animals, parrots' beaks, blood, broken bottles, feathers, egg-shells, images in wax, the hearts of birds, livers of mice, and some potent roots, weeds, and bushes, of which Europeans are at this time ignorant.

It may appear singular, that this destructive practice, so prevalent in *Jamaica,* should not have received an earlier check from the Legislature.—The fact is, the great skill of some negroes in the art of poisoning, has been noticed for a considerable time. *Sloane* and *Barham,* who practised physic in *Jamaica* in the last century, have mentioned particular instances of it. The secret and insidious manner in which the crime is generally perpetrated, makes the legal proof extremely difficult; suspicions, therefore, have been frequent, but detections rare. These murderers have sometimes been brought to justice; but it is reasonable to believe that a far greater number have escaped with impunity.

In regard to the other and more common tricks of Obi, such as hanging up feathers, bottles, eggshells, &c. &c. in order to intimidate negroes of a thievish disposition from plundering huts, hog-styes, or provision-grounds, these were laughed at by the white inhabitants, as harmless stratagems contrived by the more sagacious blacks, and serves for much the same purpose as the scare-crows which are in general used among our English farmers and gardeners. But, in the year 1760, when a very formidable insurrection of the *Koramantyn*, or Gold-coast negroes, broke out in the parish of *St. Mary,* and spread through almost every other district of the island, an old *Koromantyn* negro, the chief instigator and Oracle of the surgents in that parish, who had administered the fetish, or solemn oath, to the conspirators, and furnished them with a magical preparation, which was to render them invulnerable, was fortunately apprehended, convicted, and hung up, with all his feathers and trumperies about him. His execution struck the insurgents with a general panic, from which they never after recovered.

The examinations taken at that time first opened the eyes of the public to the very dangerous tendency of the Obeah practices, and gave birth to the law which was then enacted for their suppression and punishment: however, neither the terror of this law, the strict investigation which has ever since been made after the professors of Obi, nor the examples of those who, from time to time, have been hanged or transported for this crime, have had the desired effect. It must be inferred, therefore, that either this sect, like many others, has flourished under persecution, or that fresh supplies are annually introduced from the *African* seminaries. The baneful effects of their influence is not confined to *Jamaica* only; similar examples may be found in other West-India colonies. *Pere Labet,* in his *History of Martinico*, has noticed some which are very extraordinary.

The following Narrative, which we have had from a Planter, of *Jamaica,* a gentleman of the strictest veracity, and who is now in *London,* will serve as a farther illustration of the foregoing description of the Obeah practice, and its fatal effects:

Upon returning to *Jamaica,* (from which he had been sometime absent) in the year 1775, he found that a great number of his negroes had died during his absence, and that of such as remained alive, at least one half were debilitated, and in a very deplorable condition. The mortality continued after his arrival; two or three were frequently buried in one day; and others were taken ill, and began to decline under the same symptoms. Every means were tried, by medicines and the most careful nursing, to preserve the lives of the feeble; but in spite of all his endeavours, the depopulation went on for a twelvemonth longer, with more or less intermission, and without his being able to ascertain the real cause; though the Obeah practice was strongly suspected, as well by himself as by the Doctor and other white persons upon the plantation, as it was known to be very common in that part of the island, and particularly among the negroes of the *Popo* country. Still he was unable to verify his suspicions, because the patients constantly denied their having anything to do with persons of that order, or any knowledge of them. At length, a negress, who had been ill for sometime, came one day, and informed him, that feeling it was impossible for her to live much longer, she thought herself bound in duty, before she died, to impart a very great secret, and acquaint him with the true cause of her disorder, in hopes that the disclosure might prove the means of stopping that mischief which had already swept away such a number of her fellow-slaves.

She proceeded to say, that her step-mother, a women of the *Popo* country, about eighty years old, but still hale and active, had put Obi upon her, as she had also done upon those who had lately died; and that the old woman had practised Obi for as many years past as she could remember.

The other negroes of the plantation no sooner heard of this impeachment, than they ran in a body to their master, and confirmed the truth of it; adding, that she had carried on this business ever since her arrival from *Africa,* and was the terror of the whole neighbourhood.

Upon this, he repaired directly, with six white servants, to the old woman's house, and forcing open the door, observed the whole inside of the roof, which was of thatch, and every crevice of the walls, stuck with the implements of her trade; consisting of rags, feathers, bones of cats, and a thousand other articles. Examining farther, a large earthern pot, or jar, closely covered, was found concealed under her bed; it contained a prodigious quantity of balls of earth, or clay, of various dimensions, whitened on the outside, and variously compounded, some with hair or rags, and feathers of all forts, and strongly bound with twine; others blended with the upper section of the sculls of cats, teeth and claws, or with human and dogs teeth, and some glass beads of different colours. There were also a great many egg-shells filled with a kind of gummy substance, the qualities of which he neglected to examine, and many little bags, stuffed with a variety of articles, the particulars of which cannot, at this time, be recollected.

The hut was immediately pulled down, and, with the whole of its contents, committed to the flames, amidst the general acclamations of all his other negroes. From motives of humanity, he declined bringing the old woman to trial, under the law of the island, which would have punished her with death, but delivered her into the hands of a party of Spaniards, who, as she was not yet thought incapable of doing some trifling kind of work, were glad to accept and carry her with them to *Cuba*.

From the moment of her departure, his negroes seemed to be animated with new spirits, and the malady spread no farther among them. The total of his losses, in the course of about fifteen years preceding the discovery, and imputable solely to the Obeah practice, he estimates at least at one hundred negroes.

Having received some farther information upon this subject from another *Jamaica* gentlemen, who sat upon the trials of two criminals convicted of this practice, we shall give the same in his own words:

"In the year 1760, the influence of the professors of the Obeah art was such, as to induce a great number of the negro slaves in Jamaica to engage in the rebellion which happened in that year, and which gave rise to the law then made against the practice of Obi. Assurance was given to these deluded people that they were to become invulnerable; and in order to render them so, the Obeah men furnished them with a powder, with which they were to rub themselves.

"In the first engagement with the rebels, nine of them were killed, and many taken prisoners. Among the latter was one very intelligent fellow, who offered to disclose many important matters, on condition that his life should be spared. This being promised, he related the active part which the negroes, known among them by the name of Obeah men, had taken in promoting the insurrection; one of whom was thereupon apprehended, tried for a rebellious conspiracy, convicted, and sentenced to die. At the place of execution, so much did he rely on his own power, he bid defiance to the executioner; telling him that it was not in the power of the white people to kill him. He was hung up, and the negro spectators were greatly dismayed when they saw him expire.

"Upon other Obeah men, who were apprehended at that time, various experiments were made with electrical machines and magic lanterns, but with very little effect, except on one, who, after receiving some very severe shocks, acknowledged that his master's obi exceeded his own."

The gentleman from whom we had this account remembers having fat twice on the trials of Obeah men, who were both convicted of selling preparations, which had occasioned the death of the parties to whom they were administered; notwithstanding which, the lenity of their judges prevailed so far, that they were only punished with transportation. To prove the fact of their guilt, two witnesses were deemed necessary, with corroborating circumstances.

Having given a circumstantial account of this imaginary charm, and its mischievous tendency, we shall now return to our hero.

We have already observed that *Amalkir*, an Obeah practitioner, dwelt in the *blue mountains*.—Jack approached his cave with a reverential awe; he fought his friendship; and *Amalkir* engaged to set all the slaves of every plantation in the island in wild commotion!—Jack was charmed with the plan, and waited with impatience its execution:—he now no longer groaned beneath the heavy burthen of the day; the sweat that chased his brow, or the stripes of his cruel task-master, created no pain;—for he had a balm at heart, which checked the corroding anguish of his daily sufferings.

Two summers had now elapsed since our hero arrived at *Jamaica*; and his fellow-slaves, excited to rebellion by the Obeah-man, became firmly attached to his design. They had, by stealth, provided themselves with arms and ammunition, which they concealed in the *blue mountains*. Nothing now was wanting; and they only waited the moment to set the plantations on fire,—to plunge the revengeful dagger in the hearts of the Europeans, and lay a fertile country in waste and ruin!—Jack, in imagination, now beheld with pleasure the dreadful scene, and smiled on its horrors.

The tenth of February, 1780, at midnight, was the time resolved on by this desperate band, headed by a more desperate and determined leaders to gleam around the flaming sword of vengeance. The night before that fixed on for the execution of their intended massacre, the chiefs of the insurrection met at the cave of *Amalkir*; and it was agreed among them, that the signal for revolt should be the firing of a gun.

Thus resolving, they separated; and now the eventful moment dawned!—The expectation of the negroes, awaiting its approach, was at the pitch. At length the awful clock warned them of the time at hand, Jack listened to the solemn toll, as from the vapoured sepulchre it struck upon his ear, and gave the bloody signal, with infinite delight! His heart swelled with pleasure, and his soul presaged glorious victory!

At this moment a gun was fired, and a horrid yell ensued. The slaves were in arms; they assembled at the foot of the blue mountains; and Jack led them on to scenes of carnage!—The alarm-bell was rung; but ere the Europeans could be aroused from their torpidity, *Crawford Town* was in a blaze*. The curled smoke ascended in volumes to the sky,

---

* Now called Old Crawford Town, deserted and in ruins, the inhabitants having built another, a little distance from it, called New Crawford Town.

and mingled with the devouring flames. Screams of the defenceless and groans of the dying, drowning the echoing noise of the slaughtering guns, assailed their ears; but this, so far from softening Jack's heart, afforded him pleasure, and urged him to the slaughter!

At this juncture, a troop of *Maroon* soldiers arrived; the rebellious negroes stood their fire, and ran with fury upon the guns of their assailants, who turned their backs, and fled from the field.

It was now five o'clock, and the sun had risen; the streaks of darkness were all dispelled, and Morning beheld the havock which shameless Night had aided. Jack, now aware that the colony would proceed against them, called off his troop, and prepared for a battle.

The Governor sent five hundred choice Maroons in pursuit of those rebels. They met, and fought. The negroes, as before, rushed upon their guns; but the Maroons firing as they retreated, kept them at bay, and made great slaughter. Jack, in vain, encouraged his men; he could not rouse them to renew the combat; and they fled in every direction.

Next day, the Governor published a proclamation, offering a free pardon to such of the insurgents as would return to their duty. This had the desired effect; for they all returned, except Jack, who was still determined to harrass the Europeans.

He again repaired to the cave of *Amalkir*, who hung an Obi-horn about his neck, rare for its supposed virtues.—Dr. *Moseley*, in his *Treatise on Sugar*, says, "I saw the Obi of the famous negro robber, *Three-finger'd Jack*, this terror of *Jamaica*. The Maroon who slew him brought it to me. It consisted of a goat's horn, filled with a compound of grave-dirt, ashes, the blood of a black cat, and human fat, all mixed into a kind of paste. A cat's foot, a dried toad, a pig's tail, a slip of virginal parchment, of kid-skin, with characters marked in blood on it, were also in his Obean bag."

Thus equipped, and armed with two guns and a cutlass, Jack made the mountains his abode, and the plains beneath his scene of depredations. He fortified every access to his cave, where none dared to follow him; terrified the inhabitants; and set the civil and military power of the island at defiance, for nearly two years!

It would be tedious to enumerate all the exploits of this famous robber; we shall, therefore, only relate a few of the most prominent.

One day, as Jack was reconnoitring on the top of *Lebanus*, he beheld a negro beneath, armed, and carrying provisions. He rushed down the mountain, and attacked him. This negro (whose name was Quashee) had been an intimate of our hero's in his days of slavery; but Jack would

WILLIAM BURDETT

now acknowledge no friendship, and commanded him to deliver. The other, who was also bold and resolute, refused; JACK drew his cutlass; upon which, QUASHEE pulled a pistol from his girdle, and shot off two of his antagonist's fingers*. This enraged JACK, who now used his sword with savage fury. Quashee received several wounds; and no longer capable of maintaining the contest, he fled; while Jack took charge of the booty, and retired to his cave.

Another time, JACK having had no food for some days, he became desperate. There stood a plantation not far from *Lebanus*, the proprietor of which had given his slaves a holiday, it being his daughter's birth-day, and they were making merry. Jack beheld with gloating eye, from his retreat, the festivity of the assembled; and trusting to the terror of his name, he seized a musket, and descended. When he came near, he hid himself behind the entwined branches of a fig-tree, and taking a good aim, he shot the overseer, who presided at the feast, and who instantly fell. The negroes were struck with a general panic; and Jack made his appearance. Not one was bold enough to seize him: he held up his three-finger'd hand, and they all fell upon their faces to the ground; then seizing as much booty as he could dispose of, he fled to his cave.

The slaves recovering from their fright, ran to the Planter, and informed him of the appearance of *three-finger'd* JACK! Their master was as much surprised as themselves, though differently instigated; their surprise was mingled with excessive fear; his was excited by the daring impudence of this bold marauder, who could assume courage enough to venture before seven hundred negroes!

In a short time, Jack's same increased to such a degree, that the whole island trembled at his name; and if any evil happened, it was attributed to Jack and his obi. In the West Indies females marry very young, and sometimes very unhappily; but the cause of their unhappiness was always attributed to Jack!—Although the sins on his shoulders were sufficiently weighty, yet he was now charged very unjustly; for he was never known to molest a woman or child. Plunder was his chief aim, and revenge on the European men.

He was said to be the head of a gang of negro robbers; but this also was false; he had neither accomplice nor associate. There were a few runaway negroes near *Mount Lebanus*, the place of his retreat, whose foreheads he had crossed with some of the *magic* in his horn, and they

---

* This circumstance gave him the nick-name of THREE-FINGER'D JACK.

could not betray him. But he scorned assistance; he robbed alone; fought all his own battles; and always killed his pursuers. By his magic, he was not only the dread of the negroes, but there were many white people who believed he was possessed of some supernatural power.

He had continued his ravages for nearly a year, when Captain *Orford*, a young Englishman of good birth, and the most amiable disposition, had come over to *Jamaica*, with a party of soldiers, who were to be garrisoned there. *Rosa*, the daughter of a Mr. *Chapman*, an eminent Planter in *Maroon's Town*, had cast a favourable eye upon *Orford*, who also beheld her with the same affection. Mr. *Chapman*, who had much at heart the happiness of his daughter, and finding that *Orford* really loved her, consented to their speedy nuptials. The lovers were transported with the joyful presage of future happiness; but their joy was soon damped by an unexpected event.

Captain *Orford*, unacquainted with fear, or the true character of our hero, would frequently traverse the blue mountains, accompanied by his favourite negro boy *Tuckey*, to enjoy the breeze which lightly fanned the mountain tops. One day, thoughtless of danger, he proceeded till he came near the mouth of Jack's cave. Jack was seated upon a crag; he no sooner beheld an enemy near, than he leaped down. *Tuckey* gave a loud scream; and *Orford*, drawing his sword, made towards Jack; who smiled upon him with contempt, and lifting up his gun by the muzzle, he knocked him down with the butt-end.

Tuckey, wild with terror, fled; and Jack seizing the senseless body of *Orford*, flung it down the mountain's side. Tuckey was proceeding homeward, when a groan struck his ear; he listened—another groan succeeded; and the compassionate boy endeavoured to learn from whence they came. Winding down the intricacies of the craggy mountain, the body of Captain *Orford* arrested his step!—His master was not dead, but very much bruised, and his skull fractured. *Tuckey* raised him from the ground, and with much difficulty bore him to the plantation of Mr. *Chapman*. *Rosa* was in an agony of grief when she beheld the hapless situation of her *Orford*. She administered to his wounds, and constantly attending him in his illness, he soon recovered; for wounds are cured to a miracle, in the West Indies, in any part of the body, except the legs, where they are seldom if ever cured.

Captain *Orford* being now perfectly recovered, Mr. *Chapman*, solicitous to have the marriage solemnized, fixed the day so eagerly looked to by the young lovers; but a fresh calamity frustrated their fond hopes.

Mr. *Chapman*, to pass away the time, proposed a variety of entertainments; and the next day was appointed for a shooting-party. The morning was fine; and the company, consisting of Mr. *Chapman*, Captain *Orford* and his boy *Tuckey*, with several planters and their servants, proceeded along the banks of the *Morant* river. Coming near the bay, the game was pretty fair; and Captain *Orford* being too eager in pursuing it, he and his boy were unfortunately separated from the rest of the party. They sprung a covey of wild fowl; the Captain fired, and brought down his mark; but the bird fell upon a rock, o'ertopping the sea, and *Tuckey* ran up the cliff to save the game. JACK, who was prowling about for prey, met and recollected him, and, without farther parley, threw him into the ocean. Fortunately, a boat was failing by at the moment, and perceiving the transaction, took the poor lad on board.

JACK now observing Captain *Orford*, he levelled his gun, and shot him in the back. The Captain endeavoured to return the fire, but Jack sprung upon him, and wounded him severely with his cutlass. *Orford* fell, bathed in blood; upon which, Jack took him on his back, and conveyed him to his cave.

Mr. *Chapman* missing *Orford*, returned with his party to seek for him. They came to the bay, and saw his gun and hat lying on the ground.—Immediately suspecting the disaster, they spread an alarm, and caused instant pursuit; but JACK eluded their search.

Mr. *Chapman* returned home, absorbed in grief. On his arrival, he was met by *Tuckey*; this, for a moment assuaged his grief, hoping that *Orford* was also returned but when the boy related the disaster, his agony increased. He feared to tell his daughter the melancholy circumstance; and dreaded the discovery.

Rosa perceiving the company returning, came, with a smiling countenance, to meet them; but seeing the melancholy air of her father, she was alarmed. She enquired the cause of his dejection, and received no answer: She then eagerly asked for her beloved *Orford*, whom she now missed; but still receiving no answer, and the sorrow which appeared on every countenance, sufficiently convinced her of the cause, and she immediately sainted away.

She was borne to her chamber; where she continued several days without taking any nourishment; and her life was despaired of.—A very sudden and favourable change, however, took place, for which neither her physician nor attendants could assign a cause, and the visibly recovered!

Mr. *Chapman* was blessed by this joyful change; he saw with transport the colour again glow on the cheek of his beloved daughter; and he was resolved that the day of her recovery should be a joyful holiday to the whole plantation. Indeed, he was in general so kind to his slaves, that they all appeared happy, and loved him; the consequence of which was, that but very few of them joined in the rebellion, and his plantation was esteemed the most thriving in the island. We can assert, from experience, that if every planter in the West Indies were to follow his humane example, it would not only tend to the increase of their own private wealth, but to the good of this country at large; and it is indisputably as easy for a master to gain the love of his slaves as their hatred.

Mr. *Chapman* one morning visited the apartment of his daughter, expecting to find her much recovered; but what was his surprise, to perceive her chamber-window open, and a sheet slung out, one end of which was tied to the bed-post! Her cloathes were on the floor. For a moment he was transfixed in amaze; but perceiving a note lying on the table, he eagerly broke the seal, and read its heart-rending contents. It was as follows:

DEAR FATHER,

"Pray pardon me. No longer able to support an existence without the partner of my heart, my *Orford,* I am determined to search the mountains, and find out this *Jack*—this terror of our island. If he has a single spark of humanity, he will restore me him on whom my soul doats. Do not be uneasy on my account. If I find him not, I shall return, and die in your arms. I can with safety seek the cave of this robber, as I understand he will not molest a female. Adieu, my dear father.

ROSA CHAPMAN

This imprudent step of *Rosa's* had such an effect upon her father, that a severe and long illness ensued.

JACK having now become the terror of the whole island, and rendered himself so obnoxious by his daily depradations, that Governor *Dalling* found it necessary to apply to his Majesty, to issue his royal proclamation, offering a reward for apprehending this daring robber. Accordingly, the following proclamation was issued, dated the 12th of *December*, 1780, and 13th of *January*, 1781:

WILLIAM BURDETT

Whereas we have been informed, by our House of Assembly of this our Island of *Jamaica*, that a very desperate gang of negro Slaves, headed by a negro man Slave, called and known by the name of *Three-finger'd Jack*, hath for many months past committed several robberies, and carried off a number of negroes and other slaves on the windward Roads into the woods, and hath also committed several murders; and that repeated parties have been fitted out, and sent against the said *Three-finger'd Jack* and his gang, who have returned without being able to apprehend the said Negro, or to prevent his making head again: And whereas our House of Assembly hath requested us to give directions for issuing a proclamation, offering a reward for apprehending the said negro, called *Three-finger'd Jack*, and also a further reward for apprehending each and every negro man Slave belonging to the said gang, and delivering him or them to any Gaoler in this island: And whereas we have since received another message from our said House of Assembly, requesting us to offer an additional reward of *Two Hundred Pounds* for the apprehending, or bringing in the head, of that daring rebel, called *Three Finger'd Jack*, who hath hitherto eluded every attempt against him. We, having taken the same into our consideration, have thought fit to issue this our royal Proclamation, hereby strictly charging and commanding, and we do hereby strictly charge and command, all and every our loving subjects within our said island, to pursue and apprehend, or cause to be pursued and apprehended, the body of the said negro, called *Three-finger'd Jack*, and also of each and every negro man slave belonging to the said gang, and deliver him or them to any of the Gaolers, of this island. And we do, at the instance of our said House of Assembly, offer a reward of *One Hundred Pounds*, and, at the like instance, a further reward of *Two Hundred Pounds*, to be paid to the person or persons who shall apprehend and take the body of the said negro, called *Three-finger'd Jack;* and we do, at the instance of our House of Assembly, offer a further reward of *Five Pounds* over and above what is allowed by law, for apprehending each and every negro belonging to the said gang, and delivering him or them to any of the Gaolers of this island, to be dealt with according to law.

Witness, his Excellency *John Dalling*, Esquire,

Captain General and Governor in Chief of our said Island of Jamaica, and other the Territories theron depending in America, Chancellor and Vice Admiral of the same, at Saint Jago de la Vega, the thirteenth day of January, in the twenty-first year of our reign, Anno Dom, 1781.

JOHN DALLING,

By his Excellency's command,
R. LEWING, *Secretary*

GOD SAVE THE KING

The House of Assembly also came to the following Resolution, which was issued soon after the first proclamation:

House of Assembly, 29th December, 1780

Resolved,

THAT over and above the reward of *One Hundred Pounds,* offered by his Majesty's proclamation, for taking or killing the rebellious negro, called *Three-finger'd Jack,* the further reward of FREEDOM shall be given to any Slave that shall take or kill the said *Three-finger'd Jack;* and that the House will make good the value of such slave to the Proprietor thereof: And if anyone of his accomplices will kill the said *Three-finger'd Jack,* and bring in his head and hand wanting the fingers, such accomplice shall be entitled to his free pardon and his freedom, as above, upon due proof being made of their being the head and hand of the said *Three-finger'd Jack.*

By the House,
SAMUEL HOWEL, *Clerk of Assembly*

In consequence of those offers, two resolute and strong negroes, named QUASHEE* and SAM, both of *Scot's Hall, Maroon Town,* with a party of their townsmen, resolved to go in search of JACK. *Quashee,*

---

* Quashee was the slave who, sometime before, in a battle, had shot off Jack's two fingers.

before he set out, got himself christened, and changed his name to *James Reeder*. Accordingly, the expedition commenced.—And now, while this party are on their pursuit, we shall return to the adventurous Rosa.

The night was extremely dark when she took the resolution of descending from her chamber, to go in search of her beloved *Orford*; but she passion which preyed upon her heart superseded every other consideration. She dressed herself as a sailor boy, to secure her from violence; and thus disguised, and unintimidated, she defied the inclemency of the weather, and proceeded to the mountains,

She had heard it said that Jack's cave was near *Mount Lebanus*, somewhere among the chain of *blue Mountains*; thither, therefore, she bent her steps. Faint and weary, she was often obliged to rest herself beneath the spreading fig-tree; her tender limbs, unused to such fatigue, sunk beneath her; her lips were parched with fever; but still the hope of recovering her lover supported her re-resolution, and made her persevere with a courage rarely to be met with in her sex.

By violent exertion she climbed the craggy steep that overlooked *Old Crawford Town*, where still were visible the ravages of the fire. The evening fast approached, and the dread thunder reverberated at a short distance; the lightning flashed around; and the rain fell in torrents down the mountain's side. *Rosa* perceived a narrow dismal path, leading to a more dismal cave; and she entered the gloomy abode, where none but the robber, or wretched in mind, could dwell.—The arched vault, formed by the rough hand of nature, and the noxious vapours that assailed her, impressed her mind with the most dismal ideas.—She dreaded to proceed; yet the still more gloomy horrors that played around the cavern's mouth, impelled her to seek a refuge. She accordingly bent her steps to the interior of the cave; the chilly dew, hanging on the projected crag, dropt upon her like ice; while fear froze her heart.—She now came to the mouth of another descent, which led still deeper into the gloomy abode; and, to her infinite surprise, beheld a taper burning beneath!—She uttered a faint scream, and fell down the rocky descent into the cave, where the glimmering taper helped, in some degree, to lessen its gloom.

Rosa lay for sometime senseless; her forehead was much bruised, and her lovely tresses hung dishevelled on her face. At length she recovered to the misery of her situation; she beheld, with tortured eye, the frightful cave, which was hung around with the skeletons of turtles, aligators, and other reptiles; a sight sufficient to damp a heart, more courageous than Rosa's.

Three-finger'd Jack, into whose cave she had thus been precipitated, was out, prowling for prey. At this critical juncture he returned, and descended into the cave, by means of a ladder, while *Rosa* was viewing, with terror, the three-finger'd hand depicted on the wall. JACK no sooner beheld an European in his cave, than he seized one of his muskets, and was about to dash out her brains; when *Rosa* fell upon her knees, and exclaimed, "Mercy! Mercy! I am a woman!"—JACK dropped his weapon, and was perplexed; for although he was resolved to shew mercy to women, yet he had also determined to put to death that being who should gain a knowledge of his cave. However, after some deliberation, he made up his mind that *Rosa* should not die*; but self-preservation demanded he should confine her in the bowels of that rock her rashness had penetrated.

JACK was wearied with the fatigues of the day; and after eating of the plantain, and drinking a quantity of liquor, some of which he also placed before *Rosa*, he sunk into a sound sleep.—*Rosa* now conceived the idea of making her escape; she reconnoitred the cave; and could find no means of extricating herself, but by the way she entered. She was therefore hastening up the ladder by which Jack descended, when a dreadful groan assailed her ear: she stopped; another groan succeeded! Astonished, she turned back; and hastening to the place from whence it proceeded, she opened the door of an inner cell, and beheld her *Orford*, pale and bloody!—She gave a loud scream, and fainted. This aroused Jack, who, on discovering the cause, threatened her with death! but his passion abating, he thrust the helpless *Orford* farther into the cell, and locked the door; then taking the ladder, he ascended, and hung the key upon a projecting part of the rock, nearly twenty feet from the ground.

Rosa being now recovered, Jack seated her on a log, which served him as a chair, and tying her hands together with a long cord, one end of which he fastened to a part of the rock, and holding the other in his

---

* We have already noticed, that Jack would never molest a female: as a farther proof of which, we shall give the following authentic anecdote:—The wife of a soldier, going to a distant part of the island to see her husband, happened to meet Three-finger'd Jack, whom she did not know; but having heard so much of his depradations, and the road being unfrequented, was fearful of proceeding; she therefore begged of the supposed stranger, seeing him armed, to escort her part of the way, to prevent her being robbed by JACK; she offered to pay him for his trouble; and taking some money out of her pocket for that purpose, Jack held up his three-finger'd hand, saying, "See here; me no hurt you, good woman; put up you money; go on; you need be no fraid!"

　　　　　　　　　　　　　　　　　　　WILLIAM BURDETT

hand, he retired to his mat; placed the ladder beneath him, and again sunk into a found sleep.

Rosa was now lost to all hope; she despaired of effecting her escape, or the release of her suffering lover. However, after a short time passed in anxious thought, hope illumined her heart.—Near where she sat was placed a table, on which stood a lighted taper; and her only means of liberating herself, was to consume the cord that bound her hands. Elated with the idea, she drew the table nearer with her feet, and holding her hands over the light, burnt the cord. Now disengaged, she tied the rope to the leg of the table; and falling upon her knees, implored Heaven to aid her escape, and that of her lover.

She now turned to the cell wherein *Orford* was confined; but her heart sunk within her, when she beheld it fastened by a large padlock, the key of which she despaired of obtaining. After a long search, she cast her eye on it, and using several ineffectual efforts to get it down, she at length happened to see a long stick, with which she unhung the key, and it fell with a great noise.—JACK was aroused; but jerking the cord he held in his hand, found, as he supposed, his prisoner safe; and so renewed his slumber. *Rosa* now cautiously approached the cell of her lover, and unlocked the door. Poor *Orford* fell senseless into her arms. His wounds were not great; but he was faint for want of nourishment. She took Jack's bottle of liquor, which stood on the table, and poured some of it down *Orford*'s throat, which greatly revived him. He no sooner recognised his preserver, than he was about to make his grateful acknowledgments; but *Rosa* checked him.

Fresh obstacles again impeded the escape of the lovers. JACK had secured the ladder, and he lay beneath the mouth of his cave; but this obstacle was soon obviated. They placed the table astride him, as cautiously as possible, on which they also put the log. *Rosa* now ascended, and *Orford* followed. As he stept from the log, down tumbled the apparatus! JACK started up in fury, and fixed the ladder; but *Orford* drew it up, and left him raging like a madman, vowing their immediate destruction. He immediately climbed up the rock, and had nearly reached the top, when *Orford,* with the butt-end of a gun, not loaded, which he had taken with him, knocked him backwards. Stunned with the blow, he lay senseless; while they effected their escape, and hastened to relieve the anxiety of *Rosa*'s father; whom, on their arrival, they found confined to his bed,—Cheered, however, by the pleasure of again beholding his daughter, and her beloved

Orford, with the hope of their future happiness, he was soon restored to health.

We shall now leave the lovers preparing for their nuptials, and return to the party who set out in pursuit of JACK.

REEDER and SAM, with their townsmen, had been creeping about in the woods upwards of three weeks, blockading, as it were, the deepest recesses of the most inaccessible parts of the island, where Jack frequented; but their search was in vain. We have reason to think that Jack, by some means or other, was apprised of the search.—*Reeder* and *Sam*, therefore, tired of this mode of war, resolved to proceed by themselves in search of his retreat, and to take him by storming it, or perish in the attempt. The little boy *Tuckey*, however, being a lad of great spirit, and a good shot, solicited, and obtained permission, to accompany them.

These three accordingly left the rest of the party; from whom they had not long separated before they discovered, by impressions among the weeds and bushes, that some person must have lately passed that way. They therefore silently and cautiously followed these impressions, and soon perceived a smoke. They now prepared for war; and came upon JACK before he observed them.—He was roasting plantains by a fire on the ground, at some little distance from his cave. Turning his head round, he discovered his enemies; and snatching his guns, instantly jumped up. His looks were fierce and terrible; and he threatened them with instant death, if they did not surrender. *Reeder* undauntedly replied, that his Obi had no power over him now; for that he had been christened and his name was no longer *Quashee*. Jack knew Reeder; and as if paralysed, he let his guns fall to the ground, and drew his cutlass. *Reeder* and *Sam* were at first frightened at the fight of him; they had no retreat; and were to contend with the bravest and strongest man in the island. But JACK was also intimidated; for he had prophesied that *white Obi* would get the better of him; and he knew, from experience, that the charm would lose nothing in the hands of *Reeder*.

Without farther parley, therefore, JACK, fearful of the event, with his cutlass in his hand, threw himself down a precipice at the back of the cave. REEDER attempted to shoot him, but his gun missed fire; SAM, however, fired, and shot him in the shoulder, as he fell. REEDER, encouraged by the flight of JACK, drew his cutlass, and immediately plunged headlong down after him. The descent was nearly thirty yards, and almost perpendicular. Both of them preserved their weapons in the fall.

Having recovered their feet, they began a most dreadful combat, with all the savage fierceness of two enraged tigers. The little boy, *Tuckey*, who had been ordered to keep out of harm's way, now reached the top of the precipice, and during the fight shot Jack in the belly.

SAM took a round-about way to get to the field of action. When he arrived at the spot, JACK and REEDER had closed, and tumbled down another precipice; in which fall they both lost their weapons. SAM immediately descended after them, and also lost his cutlass among the bushes in getting down. He came just time enough to save *Reeder*, for though they were without weapons, they were not idle. JACK had caught his antagonist by the throat with a lion's grasp.—*(See the plate.)*

The combatants now presented a most horrid spectacle. REEDER had his right hand almost cut off; and JACK, whose wounds were also deep and desperate, streamed with blood from his shoulder and belly. In short, both combatants were literally covered with gore.

In this state of the battle, the little boy, *Tuckey* who was armed with a pistol and cutlass, just came up; he snapped his pistol at JACK, but it missed fire. Sam, however, was umpire, and decided the fate of the day. He struck JACK on the head with a piece of a rock. Stunned with the blow, he let go his hold, and fell senseless.

They then rushed upon him, and with *Tuckey's* cutlass cut off his head and three-finger'd hand, (both of which are at this time preserved in spirits, for the inspection of the curious) and carried in triumph to *Morant Bay*.

They there put their trophies into a pail of rum; and, followed by a vast concourse of negroes, now no longer afraid of JACK's Obi, blowing their shells and horns, and firing guns in their rude manner, they proceeded to *Kingston* and *Spanish Town*, and claimed the rewards promised by the King's proclamation and House of Assembly.

Mr. *Chapman* being perfectly recovered from his indisposition, the marriage between Captain *Orford* and the amiable *Rosa* was solemnized with the greatest festivity; the Captain sold his commission, and purchased a large plantation, near *New Crawford Town*, where they enjoyed an uninterrupted series of happiness for many years. Mr. *Chapman*, about five years after their marriage, died, and left the bulk of his fortune to Captain *Orford*, who, a short time since, was supposed to be one of the richest men in the island.

REEDER and SAM, having obtained their freedom, and the promised rewards, annually celebrate the joyful event, and the fall of the once terror of the whole island of JAMAICA—

a man, perhaps, of as genuine courage as ever existed; and who, in all probability, had he not been consigned to slavery by the base treachery of the King of Bambarra, would have been an ornament to his country.

AN

ACCURATE DESCRIPTION

OF

Obi; or, Three–Finger'd Jack.

AS PERFORMED AT THE

THEATRE-ROYAL, HAY-MARKET

Characters

Men

Three-finger'd Jack.
Captain Orford.
Tuckey, (Captain's Boy)
Planter.
Overseer.

Quashee.
Sam.
Planter's Servants.
Negro Robbers.
Jonkanoo*.

Women

Rosa, Planter's daughter.
Quashee's Wife.

Sam's Wife.
Obeah Woman.

---

* Jonkanoo is a grotesque personage, with a ludicrous false head, and head-dress, presiding as Master of the Ceremonies at negro balls in Jamaica.

Scene—*The Island of Jamaica*

Act I

Scene 1.—*A View of extensive Plantations.—The Planter's House on one side; great Gates on the other.*—Preparations are making to celebrate the birth-day of Rosa, the Planter's daughter.—Captain Orford arrives from England, and is introduced to Rosa by her father.—After a morning visit, he departs to take a walk, attended by his boy Tuckey, and speedily returns, being stunned by a blow from Three-finger'd Jack.—Rosa appears agitated.—Panic of the Slaves at the name of Jack;—and superior courage displayed by the two negroes Quashee and Sam.

Scene 2.—*An Apartment in the Planter's House.*—Captain Orford enters, much recovered from the blow he received.—He professes love to Rosa; and the Planter resolves to unite them in marriage.—A proclamation is posted up, offering a reward for the apprehension of Three-finger'd Jack.—The Planter, Orford, &c. prepare for a shooting-party.

Scene 3.—*Inside of the Obeak-woman's Cave.*—Negro robbers descend into the cave, and pay homage to the Obeah-woman, who presents them with Obi. Three-finger'd Jack suddenly enters; and is enraged at the proclamation issued against him. His obi-horn is filled by the Obeah-woman; and he uses some ceremonies to prevent the negroes from betraying him.—Dance, and carousal, of the Negroes.—An alarm.—Jack suddenly disappears in consequence of it.—The Negroes are astonished, and descend still deeper into the cave.

Scene 4.—*A Promontory, with a View of the Sea, and a Boat at Anchor.*—The Planter, Captain Orford, and Tuckey, with a shooting-party, appear.—Jack ascends from the cave, and lies in ambush. He seizes Tuckey, and casts him into the sea; then wounds Captain Orford, and carries him to his cave. The Planter appears distressed, and the Negroes terrified.

Scene 5.—*Montago Bay,*—Tuckey makes known Captain Orford's and his own adventure with Three-finger'd Jack. The Planter and his daughter Rosa are dejected, and grieved at the circumstance. Another proclamation is posted up, by the Officers of Government, for killing Three-finger'd Jack. The two negroes, Quashee and Sam, undertake to go in search of him; and are joined by Tuckey. Quashee requests to be christened, that he may overmatch Jack.

SCENE 6.—*Outside of Part of the Overseer's House, with Grounds adjacent.*—A march.—Quashee and Sam's return from the church, after the christening of the former.—Preparations for the expedition against Jack. Rejoicings of the Slaves. A negro ball.

SONGS, &c. IN ACT I

DUET.—QUASHEE's *Wife* and SAM's *Wife*

THE white man come, and bring his gold,
The slatee meet him in the bay;—
And, Oh; poor negro then be sold,—
From home poor negro sail away.

O, it be very sad to see
Poor negro child and father part!
But if white man kind massa be,
He heal the wound in negro's heart.

CHORUS of NEGROES

Good massa we find;
Sing tingering, sing terry,—
When buckra* be kind,
Then negro heart merry.
Sing tingering, &c.

OVERSEER

Black ladies and gentlemen, please to draw near,
And attend to the words of your grand Overseer.
Leave work till tomorrow, my hearts, in the morning;
Be jovial and gay, for this is the day
That our master, the good Planter's, daughter was born in.

---

* *Buckra*—a white man.

'Tis your lady's birth-day,
Therefore we'll make holiday,
And you shall all be merry,

CHORUS

Sing tingering, &c.

AIR—OVERSEER, and CHORUS

Swear by the silver crescent of the night,
Beneath whose beams the negro breathes his prayer;
Swear by your fathers slaughter'd in the fight,
By your dear native land, and children, swear;

Swear to pursue this traitor, and annoy him;
This Jack, who daily works your harms,
With Obi, and his magic charms—
Swear, swear, you will destroy him.

CHORUS of NEGROES

Kolli, kolli, kolli*! we swear all—
We kill, when he come near us;
But no swear loud—for, when we bawl,
Three-finger Jack he hear us.

DUET.—QUASHEE and WIFE

QUASHEE: Quashee he load his gun;
    Me go kill Jack, dear;
    Hill will no cover sun
    When Quashee come back, dear.
WIFE: War no be certain, and gun no be true;
    Quashee shou'd Jack kill, my heart break for you!
    Sweet music tink a tang, stay here delighting;
    No go to battle—big Death come in fighting.

---

* *Kolli*—swear.

QUASHEE: Me laugh at Obi charm—
　　Quashee strong hearted;
WIFE: Ah! me fear many harm,
　　When you and me parted.
WIFE: No go, Oh, no go, sweet Quashee, me pray?
QUASHEE: Yes, Oh, yes go, but long me no stay.

WIFE: {

Dropp so, me droop so when		you / me	far away.
Sweet / Let	music tink a tank	stay here / me no	delighting
No / Yes	go to battle	big death come / men die	in fighting

QUASH: {

FINALE

QUASHEE'S WIFE

We Negro men and women meet,
And dance and sing, and drink and eat,
With a yam foo, foo,—

And when we come to negro ball,
One funny big man be master of all;
'Tis merry Jonkanoo.

CHORUS

Now we dance, and sing, and eat,
Yam, foo, foo, with a yam foo, foo.

QUASHEE'S WIFE

Massa he poor Negro treat
Give grand ball and Jonkanoo,

CHORUS

Massa he poor Negro, &c.

WILLIAM BURDETT

Sam's Wife

Jack he did good Captain wound;
Shoot him shoulder; hurt him back.
If by Quashee Jack be found,
Then goodbye Three-finger Jack.

Chorus

Now we dance, &c.

Quashee's Wife

Jack have charm in Obi-bag;
Tom cat foot, pig tail, duck beak;
Quashee tear the charm to rag,
Make Three-finger Jack to squeak.

Chorus

Now we dance, &c.

Act II

Scene 1.—*An accurate Representation of the inside of a Slave's Hut.*—Quashee and Sam take leave of their wives and children. Rosa comes to them, in boy's clothes, and obtains their consent to accompany them on their expedition.

Scene 2.—*A Sea Beach.*—Negro robbers are seen prowling about for plunder. Three-finger'd Jack makes his appearance; they shew signs of submission to him; and he departs. The robbers are roused from their concealment by the party in quest of Jack. Jack re-enters to the robbers, who are in great awe of his Obi-horn.

Scene 3.—*A Promontory; with the mouth of Jack's Cave.*—A violent storm of rain, thunder, and lightning.—Quashee, Sam, Tuckey, and Rosa enter. Rosa appears fatigued. She enters into the cave for shelter, while the rest of the party proceed. She is shortly after followed by Jack.

Scene 4.—*A Subterranean Passage.*—Rosa is surprised by Jack. His intention of shooting her changed to making her his servant.

Scene 5.—*The Inside of Jack's Cave.*—Rosa officiates as a servant to Jack. She sings him to sleep. She then discovers Captain Orford confined in the cave, and wounded; whose escape, with her own, she effects, by stratagem.

Scene 6.—*An Apartment in the Planter's House.*—Quashee's wife is soothing the Planter with hopes of his daughter's return.

Scene 7.—*Mount Lebanus.*—A desperate fight between Jack and the party in pursuit of him. Jack's overthrow, and death.

Scene 8.—*Subterranean Passage.*—Negro robbers bring an account of Jack's death to the Obeah-woman. Capture of them by Captain Orford, Quashee, Sam, and Tuckey.

Scene last.—Public rejoicings, occasioned by the death of Three-finger'd Jack.

Songs, &c. in Act II

Song

Quashee's Wife

My cruel love to danger go,
No think of pain he give to me

Too soon me fear like grief to know
As broke the heart of Ulalee,
Poor negro woman, Ulalee!

Poor soul! to see her hang her head,
All day, beneath the cypress tree;—
And still she sing, "My love be dead—
The husband of poor Ulalee.
Poor negro woman, Ulalee!

My love be kill'd; how sweet he smil'd!
His smile again me never see;
Unless me see it in the child
That he have left poor Ulalee.
Poor negro woman, Ulalee!

My baby to my breast I fold,
But little warmth, poor boy! have he;
His father's death make all so cold
About the heart of Ulalee."
Poor negro woman, Ulalee!

Song.—Rosa

A lady, in fair Seville city,
Who once fell in love, very deep,
On her Spanish guittar play'd a ditty,
That lull'd her old guardian to sleep.
With a hoo, tira, lira, &c.

Her guardian, not giving to dozing,
Was thought the most watchful of men
But each verse had so sleepy a closing,
That he nodded—but soon 'woke again.
With a hoo, tira, &c.

She touch'd the guittar somewhat slower,
Again he look'd drowsy and wise;
And then she play'd softer, and lower,

Till, gently, she seal'd up his eyes.
With a hoo, tira, &c.

Air.—Quashee's Wife

You never hear of Mandingo* King!
He lost dear daughter, in the fight;
But she steal home to his tent, at night—
Then merry black man was Mandingo King.

Mandingo King, Oh, his heart was glad;
He call his loving subjects round—
And say, "Look here, be dear daughter found;
"Go dance to the banja†, just like mad."

The King for signal throw big dart;
Oh, then black men shout loud, and clear;
And high they jump for his daughter dear,
But none jump so high as her father's heart.

Finale

Wander now, to and fro,
Cross the wide savannahs go;
Now no fright negroes know—
Tangarang, tan tang, taro.

Beat big drum—wave fine flag;
Bring good news to Kingston town, O;
No fear Jack's Obi-bag—
Quashee knock him down, O!

Oh, through the dale, and over hill,
The negro now may go—
For charm be broke, and Jack be kill—
'Twas Quashee gave the blow.

---

* *Mandingoes* are inhabitants of certain districts in *Africa.*
† *Banja*—a rude musical instrument.

WILLIAM BURDETT

Overseer

Here we see villany
Brought, by law, to short duration;
And may all Traitors fall
By British proclamation!

Chorus

Then let us sing,
God save the King, &c.

Finis

A Note About the Author

William Burdett is the author of *The Life and Exploits of Three-Finger'd Jack: The Terror of Jamaica* (1801). While little is known about Burdett, his pamphlet is inspired by the story of Jack Mansong a. k. a. Three-Fingered Jack, an eighteenth-century leader of runaway slaves in the Colony of Jamaica. Burdett's novel went through several editions and seems to have been immensely popular in England.

A Note from the Publisher

Spanning many genres, from non-fiction essays to literature classics to children's books and lyric poetry, Mint Edition books showcase the master works of our time in a modern new package. The text is freshly typeset, is clean and easy to read, and features a new note about the author in each volume. Many books also include exclusive new introductory material. Every book boasts a striking new cover, which makes it as appropriate for collecting as it is for gift giving. Mint Edition books are only printed when a reader orders them, so natural resources are not wasted. We're proud that our books are never manufactured in excess and exist only in the exact quantity they need to be read and enjoyed.

Discover more of your favorite classics with Bookfinity™.

- Track your reading with custom book lists.
- Get great book recommendations for your personalized Reader Type.
- Add reviews for your favorite books.
- AND MUCH MORE!

Visit **bookfinity.com** and take the fun Reader Type quiz to get started.

Enjoy our classic and modern companion pairings!

www.ingramcontent.com/pod-product-compliance
Lightning Source LLC
Chambersburg PA
CBHW020321150626
46552CB00022B/3068